Thomas
Farrell
November 6, 2006

Donated by

**The Mulready Home and School
Association**

Miss Fox's Class EARNS A FIELD TRIP

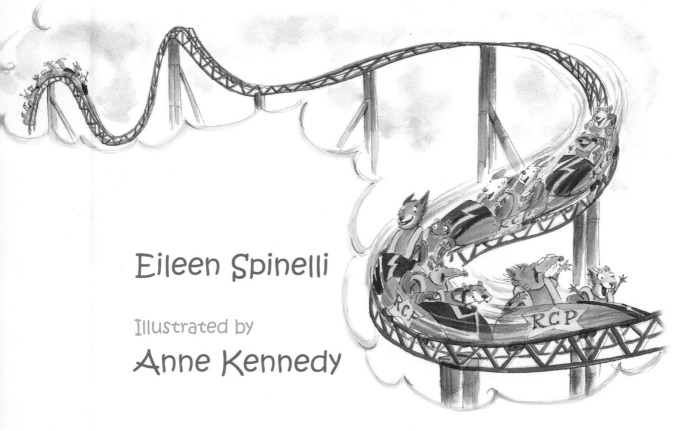

Eileen Spinelli

Illustrated by
Anne Kennedy

www.av2books.com

Your AV² Media Enhanced book gives you a fiction readalong online. Log on to www.av2books.com and enter the unique book code from this page to use your readalong.

AV² Readalong Navigation

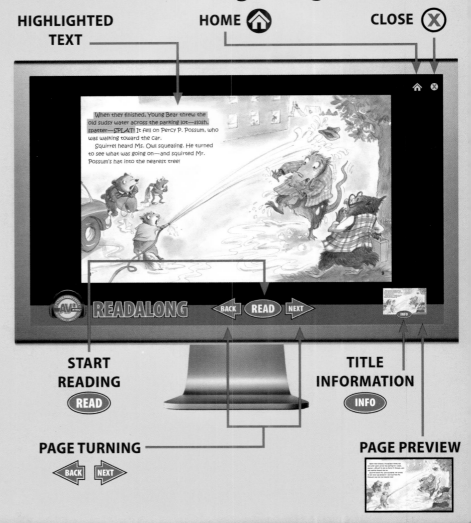

HIGHLIGHTED TEXT

HOME

CLOSE

START READING
READ

TITLE INFORMATION
INFO

PAGE TURNING
BACK NEXT

PAGE PREVIEW

Go to **www.av2books.com**, and enter this book's unique code.

BOOK CODE

E 6 2 6 0 3 5

AV² by Weigl brings you media enhanced books that support active learning.

First Published by

ALBERT WHITMAN & COMPANY

Publishing children's books since 1919

2

Published by AV² by Weigl
350 5th Avenue, 59th Floor New York, NY 10118

Copyright ©2013 AV² by Weigl

052012
WEP160512

Printed in the United States of America in North Mankato, Minnesota
1 2 3 4 5 6 7 8 9 0 16 15 14 13 12

Text copyright © 2010 by Eileen Spinelli.
Illustrations copyright © 2010 by Anne Kennedy.
Published in 2010 by Albert Whitman & Company.

Library of Congress Cataloging-in-Publication Data

Spinelli, Eileen.
 Miss Fox's class earns a field trip / by Eileen Spinelli ; illustrated by Anne Kennedy.
   p. cm.
 Summary: Students in Miss Fox's class have a series of mishaps, all involving a certain visiting author, as they try to earn money for a field trip to Roller Coaster World.
 ISBN 978-1-61913-122-4 (hard cover : alk. paper)
 [1. Moneymaking projects--Fiction. 2. School field trips--Fiction. 3. Schools--Fiction. 4. Animals--Fiction.] I. Kennedy, Anne, 1955- ill. II. Title.
 PZ7.S7566Mhm 2012
 [E]--dc23
                                          2012016741

Miss Fox brought a poster into her classroom. It said:

"FOR YOUR NEXT FIELD TRIP, VISIT ROLLER COASTER PLANET!"

"Who would like to go to Roller Coaster Planet?" Miss Fox asked.

All the students raised their hands.

Miss Fox said, "We will need $75 to rent a van to take us there. Plus $60 for tickets, for a grand total of $135."

4

She held up a big jar. "We can
save the money we earn in this."
"One hundred thirty-five dollars
is a lot of money," said Frog.
"We can do it!" said Mouse.

5

When Ms. Owl, the librarian, heard that Miss Fox's class needed money for their field trip, she gave them a job. "I'll be driving our visiting author, Percy P. Possum, home. It would be nice to take him in a clean, shiny car."

"We can wash your car!" said Young Bear.

"I will pay $20," said Ms. Owl.

At the last recess of the day, Miss Fox's class borrowed buckets and rags and soap from the school janitor and set to work.

Soon Ms. Owl's car sparkled.

When they finished, Young Bear threw the old sudsy water across the parking lot—slosh, spatter—SPLAT! It fell on Percy P. Possum, who was walking toward the car.

Squirrel heard Ms. Owl squealing. He turned to see what was going on—and squirted Mr. Possum's hat into the nearest tree!

Though the visiting author was very nice about it all, Ms. Owl had to subtract the $15 cleaning bill for Mr. Possum's suit from the $20 she had promised. So, after all that work, Ms. Fox's class earned only $5.

Mouse did the math:
"We still need $130."

That night, Mouse took out her $1.50 candy money to give to the field trip fund.

Frog found the $2 his aunt had sent from Florida.

Bunny discovered $1.50 under a chair cushion.

$$
\begin{array}{r}
1.50 \\
+\ 2.00 \\
+\ 1.50 \\
\hline
\$5.00
\end{array}
\qquad
\begin{array}{r}
5.00 \\
+\ 5.00 \\
\hline
\$10.00
\end{array}
\qquad
\begin{array}{r}
135 \\
-\ 10 \\
\hline
\$125
\end{array}
$$

Squirrel did the math—$5 from the students plus the $5 from Ms. Owl made $10. There was $125 left to earn.

Young Bear had an idea.
"Let's put on a play!
We can charge admission."

Bunny suggested they invite Mr. Possum—free of charge. "To make up for the sudsy bath," she said.

Mouse's grandmother wrote a play for the class called *Please Pass the Turnips*. All the parents helped make costumes.

Bunny and Mouse took the parts of the turnips. Squirrel was the nut. Young Bear was the pineapple, Frog, the spinach leaf, and Raccoon, the banana peel. Miss Fox directed.

The play was a great success. They sold $60 worth of tickets. Now, with the $10 already in the money jar, they had $70 altogether.

Frog shouted, "We only need $65 more!"

$$\begin{array}{r} 135 \\ -\ 70 \\ \hline \$65 \end{array}$$

But when Percy P. Possum came backstage to congratulate the cast, he slipped on Raccoon's banana peel outfit. He slid across the floor. His glasses popped off his nose—PLUNK!— into the party punch. One lens broke.

It cost $25 to repair Mr. Possum's glasses.

Later, Bunny did the math:

"$70 minus $25 equals $45 towards Roller Coaster Planet. Oh, no—now we need $90!"

70
−25
$45

135
−45
$90

It was Raccoon's idea to bake and sell brownies. Miss Fox offered her kitchen. Bunny mixed the sugar and flour. Mouse added the cocoa. Raccoon cracked the eggs. Squirrel poured the oil, and Young Bear, the water.

Each took a turn stirring the batter.

Miss Fox put the first batch of brownies in the oven to bake. That's when Raccoon shouted, "My loose tooth fell out! My tooth-fairy money! FIND MY TOOTH!"

They searched all over the kitchen, but no one found it.

19

When the brownies were finished, customers came to pick them up. There were 10 baskets for $3 each. That made $30.

A few brownies were left. Frog suggested to give Mr. Possum a basket, too. "To make up for the broken glasses." And so they did.

Mr. Possum took a brownie. "Mmmmm," he said. "This looks yummy!" He bit into it. "OUCH!"

... ssum had found Raccoon's tooth—baked ... ownie!

... Mr. Possum's own tooth had chipped.
He had to go to the dentist.

Later, Young Bear did the math. Money already earned was $45. Brownie profits were $30. That came to $75. Then he subtracted $40 for Mr. Possum's visit to the dentist. "Now we have just $35 dollars in our field trip fund," he told the group. "We still need $100."

Frog shook his head. "We can kiss Roller Coaster Planet good-bye."

"Don't give up yet," said Miss Fox. "I have good news. Principal Moose wants us to clean out his garage. He said we can sell everything—and keep the profit!"

Mr. Moose had a garage full of stuff, even a plaster bust of the famous playwright William Hog Shakespeare. The class taped price tags to the items.

Everything sold. Everything but the bust of Shakespeare.

The class made $80.

Raccoon did the math. "We're getting very close: $80 + $35 = $115. Only $20 to go!"

Frog said, "Let's give William Hog Shakespeare to Mr. Possum. Free. It would look good on his writing desk."

"It would make up for his chipped tooth," said Mouse.

They wheeled the plaster bust to Mr. Possum's house.

"We brought you a present," piped up Bunny.

Frog lifted the heavy bust out of the wagon.
He wobbled over to Mr. Possum. Then he tripped
and dropped it—CRASH!—onto
Mr. Possum's garden gnome.

"Oh, no!" cried Mr. Possum.

Miss Fox looked at the shattered gnome.
"We're so sorry," she said. "We will buy you a new
garden gnome."

"Good grief!" said Mr. Possum. "First my hat.
Then my glasses. Then my tooth.
Now my garden gnome. What next!"

Squirrel sighed. "Will we ever get to Roller Coaster Planet?"

Mr. Possum looked at the students' gloomy faces. Suddenly he didn't feel so grumpy anymore. He said, "Actually, you kids are terrific!"

"Terrific?" said Bunny. "I thought we were sad and broke."

"What makes us so terrific?" asked Raccoon.

"You never give up," replied Mr. Possum. "And that's why I will replace the broken gnome myself—with Mr. Shakespeare!"

The students cheered.

Mr. Possum thought for a moment.
"How much money do you still need
for your trip?" he asked.

"Twenty dollars," said Young Bear.

"Done!" said Mr. Possum.
"I think it's safer just to give you
the rest of the money." He took
$20 out of his wallet and gave it to
Miss Fox."

"Thank you," said Miss Fox. She put the dollars in the money jar.

Frog clapped. "Ask Mr. Possum to come with us to Roller Coaster Planet."

"Miss Fox doesn't have to ask," said Mr. Possum. "I'm coming! Roller coasters are my favorite thing!"

Miss Fox smiled. She waved the money jar. "Roller Coaster Planet—we're on our way!"